Henry Wadsworth Longfellow

Flower-De-Luce

Henry Wadsworth Longfellow

Flower-De-Luce

ISBN/EAN: 9783337105921

Printed in Europe, USA, Canada, Australia, Japan

Cover: Foto ©Andreas Hilbeck / pixelio.de

More available books at **www.hansebooks.com**

FLOWER-DE-LUCE.

BY

HENRY WADSWORTH LONGFELLOW.

WITH ILLUSTRATIONS.

BOSTON:
TICKNOR AND FIELDS.
1867.

UNIVERSITY PRESS: WELCH, BIGELOW, & CO.,
CAMBRIDGE.

CONTENTS.

LIST OF ILLUSTRATIONS.

FLOWER-DE-LUCE.

BEAUTIFUL lily, dwelling by still rivers,
　　Or solitary mere,
Or where the sluggish meadow-brook delivers
　　Its waters to the weir!

Thou laughest at the mill, the whirr and worry
　　Of spindle and of loom,
And the great wheel that toils amid the hurry
　　And rushing of the flume.

Born to the purple, born to joy and. pleasance,

    Thou dost not toil nor spin,

But makest glad and radiant with thy presence

    The meadow and the lin.

The wind blows, and uplifts thy drooping banner,

    And round thee throng and run

The rushes, the green yeomen of thy manor,

    The outlaws of the sun.

The burnished dragon-fly is thine attendant,

    And tilts against the field,

And down the listed sunbeam rides resplendent

    With steel-blue mail and shield.

Thou art the Iris, fair among the fairest,

 Who, armed with golden rod

And winged with the celestial azure, bearest

 The message of some God.

Thou art the Muse, who far from crowded cities

 Hauntest the sylvan streams,

Playing on pipes of reed the artless ditties

 That come to us as dreams.

O flower-de-luce, bloom on, and let the river

 Linger to kiss thy feet!

O flower of song, bloom on, and make forever

 The world more fair and sweet

PALINGENESIS.

I LAY upon the headland-height, and listened
  To the incessant sobbing of the sea
    In caverns under me,
And watched the waves, that tossed and fled and
    glistened,
Until the rolling meadows of amethyst
    Melted away in mist.

Then suddenly, as one from sleep, I started ;

For round about me all the sunny capes

Seemed peopled with the shapes

Of those whom I had known in days departed,

Apparelled in the loveliness which gleams

On faces seen in dreams.

A moment only, and the light and glory

Faded away, and the disconsolate shore

Stood lonely as before ;

And the wild roses of the promontory

Around me shuddered in the wind, and shed

Their petals of pale red.

There was an old belief that in the embers

Of all things their primordial form exists,

And cunning alchemists

Could recreate the rose with all its members

From its own ashes, but without the bloom,

Without the lost perfume.

Ah me! what wonder-working, occult science

Can from the ashes in our hearts once more

The rose of youth restore?

What craft of alchemy can bid defiance

To time and change, and for a single hour

Renew this phantom-flower?

"O, give me back," I cried, "the vanished
    splendors,
The breath of morn, and the exultant strife,
    When the swift stream of life
Bounds o'er its rocky channel, and surrenders
The pond, with all its lilies, for the leap
    Into the unknown deep!"

And the sea answered, with a lamentation,
Like some old prophet wailing, and it said,
    "Alas! thy youth is dead!
It breathes no more, its heart has no pulsation;
In the dark places with the dead of old
    It lies forever cold!"

Then said I, " From its consecrated cerements

I will not drag this sacred dust again,

        Only to give me pain;

But, still remembering all the lost endearments,

Go on my way, like one who looks before,

        And turns to weep no more."

Into what land of harvests, what plantations

Bright with autumnal foliage and the glow

        Of sunsets burning low;

Beneath what midnight skies, whose constellations

Light up the spacious avenues between

        This world and the unseen!

Amid what friendly greetings and caresses,

What households, though not alien, yet not mine,

What bowers of rest divine ;

To what temptations in lone wildernesses,

What famine of the heart, what pain and loss,

The bearing of what cross !

I do not know ; nor will I vainly question

Those pages of the mystic book which hold

The story still untold,

But without rash conjecture or suggestion

Turn its last leaves in reverence and good heed,

Until "The End" I read.

THE BRIDGE OF CLOUD.

BURN, O evening hearth, and waken
  Pleasant visions, as of old!
Though the house by winds be shaken,
  Safe I keep this room of gold!

Ah, no longer wizard Fancy
  Builds her castles in the air,
Luring me by necromancy
  Up the never-ending stair!

But, instead, she builds me bridges

    Over many a dark ravine,

Where beneath the gusty ridges

    Cataracts dash and roar unseen.

And I cross them, little heeding

    Blast of wind or torrent's roar,

As I follow the receding

    Footsteps that have gone before.

Naught avails the imploring gesture,

    Naught avails the cry of pain!

When I touch the flying vesture,

    'T is the gray robe of the rain.

2

Baffled I return, and, leaning

 O'er the parapets of cloud,

Watch the mist that intervening

 Wraps the valley in its shroud.

And the sounds of life ascending

 Faintly, vaguely, meet the ear,

Murmur of bells and voices blending

 With the rush of waters near.

Well I know what there lies hidden,

 Every tower and town and farm,

And again the land forbidden

 Reassumes its vanished charm.

Well I know the secret places,

    And the nests in hedge and tree ;

At what doors are friendly faces,

    In what hearts are thoughts of me.

Through the mist and darkness sinking,

    Blown by wind and beaten by shower,

Down I fling the thought I 'm thinking,

    Down I toss this Alpine flower.

HAWTHORNE.

MAY 23, 1864.

HOW beautiful it was, that one bright day
In the long week of rain!
Though all its splendor could not chase away
The omnipresent pain.

The lovely town was white with apple-blooms,
And the great elms o'erhead
Dark shadows wove on their aerial looms,
Shot through with golden thread.

Across the meadows, by the gray old manse,

    The historic river flowed :

I was as one who wanders in a trance,

    Unconscious of his road.

The faces of familiar friends seemed strange :

    Their voices I could hear,

And yet the words they uttered seemed to change

    Their meaning to my ear.

For the one face I looked for was not there,

    The one low voice was mute ;

Only an unseen presence filled the air,

    And baffled my pursuit.

Now I look back, and meadow, manse, and stream
    Dimly my thought defines;
I only see — a dream within a dream —
    The hill-top hearsed with pines.

I only hear above his place of rest
    Their tender undertone,
The infinite longings of a troubled breast,
    The voice so like his own.

There in seclusion and remote from men
    The wizard hand lies cold,
Which at its topmost speed let fall the pen,
    And left the tale half told.

Ah! who shall lift that wand of magic power,

And the lost clew regain?

The unfinished window in Aladdin's tower

Unfinished must remain!

CHRISTMAS BELLS.

I HEARD the bells on Christmas Day
Their old, familiar carols play,
    And wild and sweet
    The words repeat
Of peace on earth, good-will to men !

And thought how, as the day had come,
The belfries of all Christendom
    Had rolled along
    The unbroken song
Of peace on earth, good-will to men !

Till, ringing, singing on its way,

The world revolved from night to day,

A voice, a chime,

A chant sublime

Of peace on earth, good-will to men!

Then from each black, accursed mouth

The cannon thundered in the South,

And with the sound

The carols drowned

Of peace on earth, good-will to men!

It was as if an earthquake rent

The hearthstones of a continent,

And made forlorn

The households born

Of peace on earth, good-will to men!

And in despair I bowed my head;

" There is no peace on earth," I said;

"For hate is strong,

And mocks the song

Of peace on earth, good-will to men!"

Then pealed the bells more loud and deep:

" God is not dead; nor doth he sleep!

The Wrong shall fail,

The Right prevail,

With peace on earth, good-will to men!"

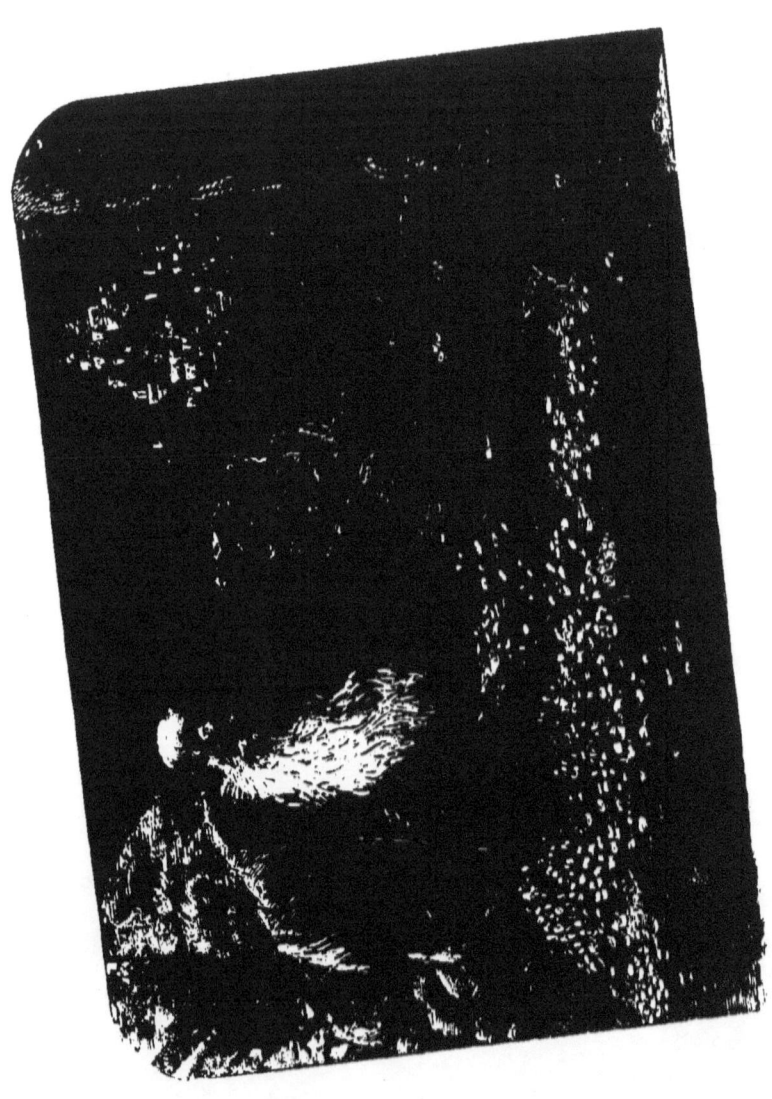

KAMBALU.

INTO the city of Kambalu,

By the road that leadeth to Ispahan,

At the head of his dusty caravan,

Laden with treasure from realms afar,

Baldacca and Kelat and Kandahar,

Rode the great captain Alau.

The Khan from his palace-window gazed,

And saw in the thronging street beneath,

In the light of the setting sun, that blazed,

Through the clouds of dust by the caravan

　　raised,

The flash of harness and jewelled sheath,

And the shining scymitars of the guard,

And the weary camels that bared their teeth,

As they passed and passed through the gates

　　unbarred

Into the shade of the palace-yard.

Thus into the city of Kambalu

Rode the great captain Alau;

And he stood before the Khan, and said:

"The enemies of my lord are dead;

All the Kalifs of all the West

Bow and obey thy least behest;

The plains are dark with the mulberry-trees,

The weavers are busy in Samarcand,

The miners are sifting the golden sand,

The divers plunging for pearls in the seas,

And peace and plenty are in the land.

" Baldacca's Kalif, and he alone

Rose in revolt against thy throne:

His treasures are at thy palace-door,

With the swords and the shawls and the jewels he

     wore ;

His body is dust o'er the desert blown.

"A mile outside of Baldacca's gate

I left my forces to lie in wait,

Concealed by forests and hillocks of sand,

And forward dashed with a handful of men

To lure the old tiger from his den

Into the ambush I had planned.

Ere we reached the town the alarm was spread,

For we heard the sound of gongs from within;

And with clash 'of cymbals and warlike din

The gates swung wide; and we turned and fled,

And the garrison sallied forth and pursued,

With the gray old Kalif at their head,

And above them the banner of Mohammed:

So we snared them all, and the town was subdued.

"As in at the gate we rode, behold,

A tower that was called the Tower of Gold!

For there the Kalif had hidden his wealth,

Heaped and hoarded and piled on high,

Like sacks of wheat in a granary;

And thither the miser crept by stealth

To feel of the gold that gave him health,

And to gaze and gloat with his hungry eye

On jewels that gleamed like ·a glow-worm's

    spark,

. Or the eyes of a panther in the dark.

"I said to the Kalif: 'Thou art old,

Thou hast no need of so much gold.

Thou shouldst not have heaped and hidden it here,

Till the breath of battle was hot and near,

But have sown through the land these useless hoards

To spring into shining blades of swords,

And keep thine honor sweet and clear.

These grains of gold are not grains of wheat;

These bars of silver thou canst not eat ;

These jewels and pearls and precious stones

Cannot cure the aches in thy bones,

Nor keep the feet of Death one hour

From climbing the stairways of thy tower!'

"Then into his dungeon I locked the drone,

And left him to feed there all alone

In the honey-cells of his golden hive:

Never a prayer nor a cry nor a groan

Was heard from those massive walls of stone,

Nor again was the Kalif seen alive!

"When at last we unlocked the door,

We found him dead upon the floor;

The rings had dropped from his withered
     hands,

His teeth were like bones in the desert sands;

Still clutching his treasure he had died;

And as he lay there, he appeared

A statue of gold with a silver beard,

His arms outstretched as if crucified."

This is the story, strange and true,

That the great captain Alau

Told to his brother the Tartar Khan,

When he rode that day into Kambalu

By the road that leadeth to Ispahan.

THE WIND OVER THE CHIMNEY.

SEE, the fire is sinking low,
Dusky red the embers glow,
  While above them still I cower,
  While a moment more I linger,
  Though the clock, with lifted finger,
    Points beyond the midnight hour.

Sings the blackened log a tune

Learned in some forgotten June

From a school-boy at his play,

When they both were young together,

Heart of youth and summer weather

Making all their holiday.

And the night-wind rising, hark!

How above there in the dark,

In the midnight and the snow,

Ever wilder, fiercer, grander,

Like the trumpets of Iskander,

All the noisy chimneys blow!

Every quivering tongue of flame

Seems to murmur some great name,

Seems to say to me, "Aspire!"

But the night-wind answers, "Hollow

Are the visions that you follow,

Into darkness sinks your fire!"

Then the flicker of the blaze

Gleams on volumes of old days,

Written by masters of the art,

Loud through whose majestic pages

Rolls the melody of ages,

Throb the harp-strings of the heart.

And again the tongues of flame

Start exulting and exclaim:

"These are prophets, bards, and seers;

In the horoscope of nations,

Like ascendant constellations,

They control the coming years."

But the night-wind cries: "Despair!

Those who walk with feet of air

Leave no long-enduring marks;

At God's forges incandescent

Mighty hammers beat incessant,

These are but the flying sparks.

"Dust are all the hands that wrought ;

Books are sepulchres of thought ;

The dead laurels of the dead

Rustle for a moment only,

Like the withered leaves in lonely

Churchyards at some passing tread."

Suddenly the flame sinks down ;

Sink the rumors of renown ;

And alone the night-wind drear

Clamors louder, wilder, vaguer, —

"'T is the brand of Meleager

Dying on the hearth-stone here ! "

And I answer, — "Though it be,

Why should that discomfort me?

No endeavor is in vain ;

Its reward is in the doing,

And the rapture of pursuing

Is the prize the vanquished gain."

THE BELLS OF LYNN,

HEARD AT NAHANT.

O CURFEW of the setting sun! O Bells of
Lynn!

O requiem of the dying day! O Bells of
Lynn!

From the dark belfries of yon cloud-cathedral
wafted,

Your sounds aerial seem to float, O Bells of
Lynn!

Borne on the evening wind across the crimson

twilight,

O'er land and sea they rise and fall, O Bells of

Lynn!

The fisherman in his boat, far out beyond the

headland,

Listens, and leisurely rows ashore, O Bells of

Lynn!

Over the shining sands the wandering cattle

homeward

Follow each other at your call, O Bells of

Lynn!

The distant lighthouse hears, and with his flaming

signal

Answers you, passing the watchword on, O Bells

of Lynn !

And down the darkening coast run the tumultuous

surges,

And clap their hands, and shout to you, O Bells

of Lynn !

Till from the shuddering sea, with your wild

incantations,

Ye summon up the spectral moon, O Bells of

Lynn !

And startled at the sight, like the weird woman of

    Endor,

Ye cry aloud, and then are still, O Bells of

    Lynn!

KILLED AT THE FORD.

H E is dead, the beautiful youth,
The heart of honor, the tongue of truth,
He, the life and light of us all,
Whose voice was blithe as a bugle-call,
Whom all eyes followed with one consent,
The cheer of whose laugh, and whose pleasant
    word,
Hushed all murmurs of discontent.

Only last night, as we rode along

Down the dark of the mountain gap,

To visit the picket-guard at the ford,

Little dreaming of any mishap,

He was humming the words of some old song :

" Two red roses he had on his cap

And another he bore at the point of his sword."

Sudden and swift a whistling ball

Came out of a wood, and the voice was still ;

Something I heard in the darkness fall,

And for a moment my blood grew chill ;

I spake in a whisper, as he who speaks

In a room where some one is lying dead ;

But he made no answer to what I said.

We lifted him up to his saddle again,

And through the mire and the mist and the rain

Carried him back to the silent camp,

And laid him as if asleep on his bed ;

And I saw by the light of the surgeon's lamp

Two white roses upon his cheeks,

And one, just over his heart, blood-red !

And I saw in a vision how far and fleet

That fatal bullet went speeding forth,

Till it reached a town in the distant North,

Till it reached a house in a sunny street,

Till it reached a heart that ceased to beat

Without a murmur, without a cry ;

And a bell was tolled in that far-off town,

For one who had passed from cross to crown,

And the neighbors wondered that she should die.

GIOTTO'S TOWER.

HOW many lives, made beautiful and sweet

By self-devotion and by self-restraint,

Whose pleasure is to run without complaint

On unknown errands of the Paraclete,

Wanting the reverence of unshodden feet,

Fail of the nimbus which the artists paint

Around the shining forehead of the saint,

And are in their completeness incomplete!

4

In the old Tuscan town stands Giotto's tower,

　　The lily of Florence blossoming in stone, —

　　A vision, a delight, and a desire, —

The builder's perfect and centennial flower,

　　That in the night of ages bloomed alone,

　　But wanting still the glory of the spire.

TO-MORROW.

'TIS late at night, and in the realm of sleep
    My little lambs are folded like the flocks;
    From room to room I hear the wakeful clocks
    Challenge the passing hour, like guards that keep

Their solitary watch on tower and steep;
    Far off I hear the crowing of the cocks,
    And through the opening door that time un-
      locks
    Feel the fresh breathing of To-morrow creep.

To-morrow! the mysterious, unknown guest,

    Who cries to me : "Remember Barmecide,

    And tremble to be happy with the rest."

And I make answer : "I am satisfied ;

    I dare not ask ; I know not what is best ;

    God hath already said what shall betide."

DIVINA COMMEDIA.

DIVINA COMMEDIA.

I.

OFT have I seen at some cathedral door

A laborer, pausing in the dust and heat,

Lay down his burden, and with reverent feet

Enter, and cross himself, and on the floor

Kneel to repeat his paternoster o'er;

Far off the noises of the world retreat;

The loud vociferations of the street

Become an undistinguishable roar.

So, as I enter here from day to day,

    And leave my burden at this minster gate,

    Kneeling in prayer, and not ashamed to pray,

The tumult of the time disconsolate

    To inarticulate murmurs dies away,

    While the eternal ages watch and wait.

II.

HOW strange the sculptures that adorn these
towers!

This crowd of statues, in whose folded sleeves

Birds build their nests; while canopied with
leaves

Parvis and portal bloom like trellised bowers,

And the vast minster seems a cross of flowers!

But fiends and dragons on the gargoyled eaves

Watch the dead Christ between the living
thieves,

And, underneath, the traitor Judas lowers!

Ah! from what agonies of heart and brain,

What exultations trampling on despair,

What tenderness, what tears, what hate of

wrong,

What passionate outcry of a soul in pain,

Uprose this poem of the earth and air,

This mediæval miracle of song!

III.

I ENTER, and I see thee in the gloom

Of the long aisles, O poet saturnine!

And strive to make my steps keep pace with

thine.

The air is filled with some unknown perfume;

The congregation of the dead make room

For thee to pass; the votive tapers shine;

Like rooks that haunt Ravenna's groves of

pine

The hovering echoes fly from tomb to tomb.

From the confessionals I hear arise

Rehearsals of forgotten tragedies,

And lamentations from the crypts below;

And then a voice celestial, that begins

With the pathetic words, "Although your sins

As scarlet be," and ends with "as the snow."

IV.

I LIFT mine eyes, and all the windows blaze
      With forms of saints and holy men who died,
      Here martyred and hereafter glorified ;
      And the great Rose upon its leaves displays
Christ's Triumph, and the angelic roundelays,
      With splendor upon splendor multiplied ;
      And Beatrice again at Dante's side
      No more rebukes, but smiles her words of
      praise.

And then the organ sounds, and unseen choirs

    Sing the old Latin hymns of peace and love,

    And benedictions of the Holy Ghost ;

And the melodious bells among the spires

    O'er all the house-tops and through heaven

        above

    Proclaim the elevation of the Host !

V.

O STAR of morning and of liberty!

O bringer of the light, whose splendor shines

Above the darkness of the Apennines,

Forerunner of the day that is to be!

The voices of the city and the sea,

The voices of the mountains and the pines,

Repeat thy song, till the familiar lines

Are footpaths for the thought of Italy!

Thy fame is blown abroad from all the heights,

    Through all the nations, and a sound is

        heard,

    As of a mighty wind, and men devout,

Strangers of Rome, and the new proselytes,

    In their own language hear thy wondrous

        word,

    And many are amazed and many doubt.

NOËL

Envoyé à M. Agassiz, la veille de Noël 1864, avec un panier de vins divers.

5

L'Académie en respect,

Nonobstant l'incorrection,

A la faveur du sujet,

    Ture-lure,

N'y fera point de rature ;

Noël ! ture-lure-lure.

              GUI-BARÔZAI.

NOËL.

QUAND les astres de Noël

Brillaient, palpitaient au ciel,

Six gaillards, et chacun ivre,

Chantaient gaîment dans le givre,

" Bons amis

Allons donc chez Agassiz ! "

Ces illustres Pèlerins

D'Outre-Mer adroits et fins,

Se donnant des airs de prêtre,

A l'envi se vantaient d'être

"Bons amis

De Jean Rudolphe Agassiz!"

Œil-de-Perdrix, grand farceur,

Sans reproche et sans pudeur,

Dans son patois de Bourgogne,

Bredouillait comme un ivrogne,

"Bons amis,

J'ai dansé chez Agassiz!"

Verzenay le Champenois,

Bon Français, point New-Yorquois,

Mais des environs d'Avize,

Fredonne à mainte reprise,

"Bons amis,

J'ai chanté chez Agassiz!"

A côté marchait un vieux

Hidalgo, mais non mousseux ;

Dans le temps de Charlemagne

Fut son père Grand d'Espagne!

"Bons amis

J'ai diné chez Agassiz!"

Derrière eux un Bordelais,

Gascon, s'il en fut jamais,

Parfumé de poésie

Riait, chantait, plein de vie,

"Bons amis,

J'ai soupé chez Agassiz!"

Avec ce beau cadet, roux,

Bras dessus et bras dessous,

Mine altière et couleur terne,

Vint le Sire de Sauterne;

"Bons amis,

J'ai couché chez Agassiz!"

Mais le dernier de ces preux,

Était un pauvre Chartreux,

Qui disait, d'un ton robuste,

"Bénédictions sur le Juste !

Bons amis

Bénissons Père Agassiz !"

Ils arrivent trois à trois,

Montent l'escalier de bois

Clopin-clopant ! quel gendarme

Peut permettre ce vacarme,

Bons amis,

A la porte d'Agassiz !

"Ouvrez donc, mon bon Seigneur,

Ouvrez vite et n'ayez peur ;

Ouvrez, ouvrez, car nous sommes

Gens de bien et gentilshommes,

Bons amis

De la famille Agassiz ! "

Chut, ganaches ! taisez-vous !

C'en est trop de vos glouglous ;

Épargnez aux Philosophes

Vos abominables strophes !

Bons amis,

Respectez mon Agassiz !